So, I'm just dumb in school, but I'm a really good gymnast.

I'd be rich if I had a dollar for every time I've heard the words, "Jodi lacks discipline." Before Patrick, even my gymnastics coaches used to complain about my lack of discipline. But with Patrick I have such a good time that I can see I'm picking up tricks quicker than ever before. It's the most fun I've had in gymnastics since I was a little kid, and I'm getting good. I can live with the fact that I'm stupid in school. School isn't everything. There's always gymnastics.

**Look for these and other books
in the GYMNASTS series:**

THE GYMNASTS

#3 NOBODY'S PERFECT

Elizabeth Levy

AN
APPLE
PAPERBACK

SCHOLASTIC INC.
New York Toronto London Auckland Sydney

ISBN 0-590-41564-6

12 11 10 9 8 7 6 5 4 3 2 1   8 9/8 0 1 2 3/9

Printed in the U.S.A.   11

First Scholastic printing, November 1988

For Ona and Isa, my godchildren, with love.

Jodi: Gymnast in Space or Space Cadet?

Patrick, my gymnastics coach, is always telling us to picture an imaginary line for our tumbling runs. There is a very real, blue, painted line in the middle of the hallway of my school. Every time I see it I want to do a cartwheel on it. We were on our way back to class from the cafeteria, and I was last in line. I let a little space get between me and the kid in front of me. Then I did a cartwheel.

I didn't realize that the second grade kids were behind me. They burst into giggles and applause.

"I give her a 9.9," said one little kid who

couldn't have been more than seven years old.

I flashed him a grin and my winning salute.

My teacher, Ms. Assante, turned around and glared at me.

"Jodi!" she said. "This is a hallway, not a gymnasium."

"Sorry," I mumbled. "I couldn't help myself. Gymnastics makes you do weird things." The kids in my class laughed, particularly my teammates Lauren and Cindi. Everyone knows we do gymnastics. I like to make the kids laugh, particularly Lauren and Cindi. They've been tight forever, it seems. They've known each other practically since they were born. I just moved to Denver from St. Louis last year.

It's not exactly that Cindi and Lauren are a clique and don't let me in. I think they like me. I think they like me a lot. It's just that both of them would say the other is their best friend, not me.

After school we all take gymnastics at Patrick's gym, the Evergreen Gymnastics Academy. Darlene is the fourth girl in our group. Darlene goes to private school, but she's not a snob. Patrick calls us the Pinecones. The rest of the Pinecones think that I have the advantage because my mom is the assistant coach at Patrick's gym. Some people think my family is like one of those circus families — gymnastics is in our blood.

Maybe they're right. Mom and Dad met doing gymnastics at college. It didn't keep them together. They're divorced, and Dad still lives in St. Louis where he runs a gymnastics center. I miss him.

Then there's my sister Jennifer. Jennifer (she's never been called Jenny) does gymnastics for the U.S. Air Force Academy. That's quite a combination. She wants to be an astronaut. She figures all that tumbling will help her in space. With my grades, I've got as much chance of being an astronaut as I've got flying to the moon. Get it? That's a joke. Unless you're an astronaut, your chances of flying to the moon are zilch. But gymnasts in space. I like it. Just imagine how easy it would be to do all our tricks if we were weightless. I could do a tumbling run that never stopped.

Cindi, Lauren, and I are in the fifth grade at P.S. 64. We're the oldest kids in the school. Next year we go to middle school. We're supposed to be an example to the younger kids, and that's why I was in trouble. Ms. Assante definitely did not like me doing a cartwheel in the hall, especially in front of the second-graders, who are a rowdy bunch. If she could, she'd send me back to second grade. I'm not exactly the class brain.

"You are in school, not gymnastics," Ms. Assante said. "Please remember it."

I wasn't likely to forget it.

I took my seat in class. I started the year in the back, and every month I've moved up so that now I sit in the front row. It's not exactly an honor. Ms. Assante decided she wanted me where she could keep an eye on me.

Ms. Assante shuffled the papers on her desk. "Would you please take out your homework assignments?" she said. "I'd like to hear a few out loud before you hand them in." Our homework assignment had been to write an essay on Colorado's ghost towns, pretending we were silver miners who had gone broke. I'm not very good at pretending.

"Jeffrey, would you share your paper with us?" Ms. Assante asked.

Jeffrey's paper went on forever about the snow seeping into the miner's cabin because he didn't have any money to pay to keep his cabin repaired. He wrote about how the miner's little baby died from the cold, and how the miner had to dig through the cold, frozen ground to bury his baby. He practically had the whole class in tears, but personally I thought it was a little morbid.

"Excellent," said Ms. Assante when he finished. She looked around the room for the next person to call on.

I sunk down low in my seat. One thing I hate about being in the front is that there's no place to hide. I hadn't really done the homework assignment. By the time I had gotten home from gymnastics yesterday I hadn't been in the mood. Besides, Thursday's my favorite television night and I had lied to my mom and told her I didn't have any homework. Then I had tried to write the essay in the morning on the bus. I had only written one sentence.

"Jodi?" asked Ms. Assante. "Could you share with us?"

I hate that word "share."

I coughed. "You may not like it," I said, turning several shades of red, "but I honestly thought this was how a miner would feel."

"Why don't you let us judge for ourselves?"

"Okay," I said with a sigh. "Spent the whole day digging and am too tired to write," I read. "The End."

The class cracked up. Ms. Assante didn't.

"Very imaginative," she said. "Jodi, would you

please see me after class?" It wasn't really a question.

"I can't," I said. "I have to be at gymnastics at three-thirty."

"I think what we have to discuss is a little more important than gymnastics," said Ms. Assante.

"Maybe to you it is," I said before I realized what was coming out of my mouth. That happens to me a lot. I say something before I think, and then I'm in trouble. But it was the truth. That was how I felt. I liked gymnastics a lot more than school, and I was better at gymnastics than I was at writing about stupid miners.

Ms. Assante was definitely angry. "You will see me after class," she insisted.

I slumped in my seat and looked out the window. Piles of snow were melting in the sun. I could barely see the mountains in the distance.

The bell rang, signaling the end of the day. Ms. Assante shuffled more papers on her desk. Lauren and Cindi came up to me.

"We'll tell Patrick and your mom you're going to be late," whispered Lauren. Lauren is absolutely never in trouble in school. "Don't give Ms. Assante a hard time," she advised me.

Cindi patted me on the head, like her puppy, but I knew she meant it to be encouraging.

"Just be sweet," whispered Cindi.

I tried to grin, but I didn't think Ms. Assante would be fooled by any last-minute sweetness act on my part. I had a feeling I was in real trouble this time.

Monkeys Don't Care About School

Ms. Assante looked up from her desk. "Cindi and Lauren?" she said. "School's over." She made it very clear that she wanted them to go. Whatever she had to say to me, she didn't want my friends around. That was not a good sign.

"I'm sorry, Ms. Assante," said Lauren. "I was just saying good-bye to Jodi."

"She's not going to jail," said Ms. Assante with a smile. "I won't keep her forever. Please close the door behind you."

Cindi and Lauren left silently. I hate being alone in the room with a teacher.

Ms. Assante came over and sat down in one of the chairs next to me. It was too little for her.

She had my notebook in her hand. I knew what was coming. She didn't open the notebook. "Jodi, what you read today in class was amusing."

I perked up. "And probably accurate," I said.

Ms. Assante nodded. "But the assignment was to write a page."

"My miner fell asleep before he could finish," I said, hoping she'd like my half-hearted joke. I wanted to play the amusing angle for all it was worth. I figured it was the only hope I had.

"However, I do not find your journal amusing," she said, pointing to my notebook.

"Uh, Ms. Assante. . . ." I looked at my watch. "I really do have to be at gymnastics. You know my mom works at Patrick's gym. She'll be worried, too."

Ms. Assante put her hand on my forearm. "Jodi, we have to talk about your journal."

"I thought it wasn't supposed to be graded," I argued. Ms. Assante is a nut about writing. I mean, she wants us to do it every day. We have to keep a journal, and she tells us that she won't grade it. But we have to turn it in every week just to prove that we're keeping it. I hate it. I can never think of what to say, and I just don't have the time. I'm at gymnastics at least three days a week after school from three-thirty to five. I'd much rather do flips than write "Today I felt like an elephant." Ms. Assante loves it when you tell her what animal you feel like. I'd never be a fish. Fish have to swim in schools. I'd be a monkey. Monkeys don't care about school and neither do I.

Ms. Assante opened my journal to my last entry. I knew she wouldn't like it. "Was this supposed to be funny?" she asked. I don't think she wanted to know the answer. I did think it was kind of funny. I had written:

TODAY . . .
                        IS . . .
                                        TUSDAY. . . .

It filled the whole page. "That's all I could think of to write," I said.

"You even spelled Tuesday wrong," said Ms. Assante.

"You said we weren't being graded."

"You are not being graded, not on your journal. But Jodi, everything you write is marred by carelessness, slipshod errors, and spelling mistakes."

"So, I'm just dumb in school," I said sticking my feet out in front of me. "But I'm a really good gymnast."

"You are not dumb," insisted Ms. Assante. "First of all, dumb refers to people or animals who can't speak. I've never noticed that you've had any problem interrupting my class to make a joke."

"Okay, I'm not dumb, just stupid." I sighed. I didn't want Ms. Assante to be my enemy. "Look, Ms. Assante. It's not just you. I've never done good in school. Even before I moved here. Face it, you've got a stupid student. I can't be your first."

"The correct grammar is: 'I've never done well in school,'" Ms. Assante said. "I would never label you stupid, Jodi. I am troubled by your lack of discipline."

I tried hard not to groan. I'd be rich if I had a dollar for every time I heard the words, "Jodi lacks discipline." Before Patrick, my gymnastics coaches used to complain about my lack of discipline. But I love to fly and run. Monkeys are great gymnasts and you never hear people complain about *their* lack of discipline. I should have been born a monkey.

I should have been paying more attention to Ms. Assante. She was droning on and on and when I picked up what she was saying, I realized I was in deep trouble. "You refuse to try in school," she said. "I'm giving you a note for your mother. I'd like her, and you, to come see me. Perhaps the three of us can come up with a solution to your problem."

"My mom's very busy," I said. "I don't think she'll have time. She works after school."

Ms. Assante gave me that look adults get when they've had enough. She took out a fountain pen and wrote a note to my mother. Then she put it in an envelope. She didn't seal it. I guess she wanted me to read it. She handed it to me. "I'd like you and your mother to come see me as soon as possible."

That's just what I needed. Have you ever noticed how teachers and adults never like to face facts? I mean, I can live with the fact that I'm stupid in school, so why can't they?

But school isn't everything. There's always gymnastics. I've lived with two great gymnasts, my mom and my sister Jennifer. Really great gymnasts aren't necessarily fearless. They're careful and disciplined. Two things that Ms. Assante would love. Two things I'm not. But with Patrick I have such a good time that I can see I'm picking up tricks quicker than ever before. It's the most fun I've had in gymnastics since I was a little kid, and I'm getting good.

Before Patrick, gymnastics for me was a little like going to school for Lauren. It was the place where my parents worked. Lauren's mom works for the Denver Board of Education, and her dad's a high school principal. At Patrick's gym, the others leave school and parents behind. Not me. It's hard for me having my mom there. She has a rule never to coach me herself, and she tries to be good about not making me feel like she's watching me. But I know she's there. Back in St. Louis, I never used to like to practice gymnastics much.

Oh, I picked it up okay, but I've never been as good as my sister. I mean, it would be impossible to be born into my family and *not* do gymnastics. But as everyone who is ever around me for more than five minutes can tell you, I don't have discipline. Even Jennifer says that about me, and I like my sister. She's almost nine years older than me, and we don't fight the way Cindi does with her brothers, or the way Darlene does with her sisters.

I think my kindergarten teacher was the first one to send out the battle cry, "Jodi lacks discipline."

It's funny, but Patrick has never used that line on me.

3

An Important Announcement

I arrived at Patrick's late and in a foul mood. I quickly changed into my leotard and went out to do my warm-ups.

Mom gave me a worried look when she saw me. She was working with the little kids on the beam. She had six of them perched on the beam together. They looked like a flock of baby birds afraid to fly. I don't ever remember being afraid to jump on and off the beam.

"Hi, honey," said Mom. "Why were you late? Was there a problem at school?"

"No prob . . . " I muttered. "Talk to you later." I didn't want to give her the note now. I was anxious to get back with the Pinecones. Darlene,

Cindi, and Lauren were sitting in a circle with some of the better gymnasts. The Pinecones are mostly intermediates. There is another group that is slightly more advanced. We're all on the same team, and you'd think we'd be allies. But they treat us like we're pond scum. I think it's because their leader, Becky Dyson, is a real pill. But the truth is that most of her friends are just as bad. Maybe like attracts like. A new girl, Ashley, just started working out with Patrick. She's tiny. She's only nine years old, but she's incredibly good. Within days, she started acting like Becky. Becky seems to be a contagious disease.

Darlene made room for me in the circle around Patrick. Her dad is Big Beef Broderick, the lineman for the Denver Broncos. Everyone in Denver loves Big Beef, and I'm not talking about the hamburger. Everyone who meets Darlene wants to be her friend. You'd think she'd be stuck up, being so rich and actually famous, but she isn't.

Patrick had one of his gymnastics books open to a page with stick figures on it. As far as I was concerned, the books never made much sense. Patrick nodded to me. "Sorry I'm late," I said. "I couldn't help it."

"Okay," Patrick said. "I'm glad you made it. We're working on back somies." A somie is a back somersault through the air. An ordinary back somersault is one you do rolling on the mat. A back somie means that you have to fly. I didn't know how to do one yet, but my handsprings were really good. I rarely needed a spot on one.

Patrick did the move for us. He got tremendous power from his run, and amazing height before he did the back somersault.

"I can already do that," said Ashley.

"Okay," said Patrick. "Let me see what you can do."

Ashley got up. She did it perfectly. She was so tiny she really flew through the air. She didn't even need Patrick to spot her.

"Isn't there anything that little twerp can't do?" whispered Darlene.

"She can't be an original Pinecone," I said.

"That's because she's so good," muttered Lauren.

"Jodi," said Patrick. "Your turn."

"Great," I said. I went to the edge of the mat to start from a run the way Ashley had done.

"I don't want you to try what Ashley did," Patrick said.

Ashley gave me a smug look. She was just a little Becky-in-training.

"Jodi, don't do the full somersault, just start from a standing position. I'll help you through it."

"She needs all the help she can get," said Becky.

Ashley snickered.

I stood up. I felt Patrick's hand on the back of my knees. "Spring up," he commanded. Just the pressure of his hand reminded me not to bend down too far. I swept my hands up, and tucked my knees to my chest. Patrick lifted me around. He needed all his strength, because I didn't have enough momentum.

"Good," said Patrick. "Very good. Could you tell why it's different from a handspring?"

"You don't sit back," I said.

"Exactly," said Patrick. "That's the exact difference. Very smart."

"I don't get it," said Lauren, scratching her head.

Patrick worked with the others. I couldn't wait to try it again. Gymnastics makes me feel like moving, and it's hard to wait while the other kids get their turns. I didn't get a chance to try the back somersault again that day. Mom's group wanted to work on the floor mats.

"Let's work on the bars," said Patrick. "Jodi, I'll take you first." I had a feeling that Patrick knew I was getting restless. That's why I like Patrick. He can read my moods, but he never makes me feel bad for being moody.

I was swinging on the high bar and doing a half turn. It takes longer to describe than to do. I love to move fast on the bars. I make mistakes, but I love the feeling of really whipping around, using gravity to make myself fly.

Suddenly I dropped down to the mats. I held my hand. I had ripped one of the calluses on my palm. It began to bleed, and it hurt like the dickens.

Patrick leaned over me. "Does it smart?"

I tried to lick the blood. "Not too bad." I grimaced. Ripping your calluses really does hurt.

"Go wash it off," he said. He put his arm around my shoulder. "You had a good workout."

I felt good. Now why couldn't school be as good as here? Maybe I should start a petition to get Patrick as a teacher. I liked that idea.

When I came back from taking care of my rip, Patrick called everyone together again. "I've got an important announcement," he said.

Becky's best friend Gloria pushed me aside so that she and Becky could sit next to Patrick.

"Listen up, kids," said Patrick. "I've got some exciting news. I've been invited to give a coaching demonstration at the U.S. Olympic Center in Colorado Springs. They are having a three-day mini-camp. Different clubs from around the state will be coming. There will be meets, but the emphasis will not be on competition but on sharing."

I grimaced. There was that word again. But Colorado Springs! It would be great. I'd have a chance to see my sister, and strut my stuff. I had improved incredibly since working with Patrick. Jennifer was used to thinking of me as a kid who would try anything, but not always succeed. Going to Colorado Springs, I'd be able to show my sister just how good I was now. It would be great.

"Jodi," said Patrick. "Are you with us?"

"Huh?"

"You looked like you were in outer space," he said. Funny how Patrick could say things like that and it didn't bother me.

"It's just Jodi, our resident space cadet," I heard Becky whisper to Ashley.

I blushed. Becky definitely *did* bother me.

"Anyhow," continued Patrick. "The emphasis will be on sharing skills. Different coaches will demonstrate techniques with their students. A lot of the groups will be better than we are. It's a three-day conference, and since schools across the state have different spring vacations, they just picked three days in March. I know some of you will have to miss a day of school. I think it will be worth it, but of course, it's up to your parents. I've written a letter to them explaining the conference and the cost. Each of you will need to bring back a signed permission slip. If your parents have any questions, just have them give me a call."

"I've got a question," said Becky. "How do we get there? Do our parents drive us?"

"No," said Patrick. "Depending on how many girls go, we'll take my van or else the minibus."

"Oh, no," said Becky, turning to Ashley. "Have you ever driven in a car with Lauren? She gets carsick going to the mall. I've driven with her once. Once was enough."

Lauren blushed. She does get carsick pretty easily.

"Becky," said Patrick, sharply. "I will have none of that pettiness and cattiness on this trip. If you cannot control that kind of sniping, I don't want you on this trip."

Becky looked embarrassed. I liked the way Patrick had told her off. She is probably one of Patrick's best gymnasts, and a lot of people think she gets special treatment because of it. But I think Patrick's fair.

Patrick handed out the notes. "This is going to be so neat," said Lauren. "I hope I can talk my parents into letting me go." Lauren's dad is a high school principal, and her mom is on the

Board of Ed. They aren't into gymnastics. It's like they're proud of Lauren and all, but they're pretty strict about not letting her miss school for any gymnastics activities.

"I'm gonna tell my parents it's an educational experience," said Darlene, when Patrick handed her the note. "I've never been to Colorado Springs."

"You're kidding," said Cindi. "It's neat down there. The Air Force Academy is beautiful. I bet we can get Jodi's sister to give us a private tour."

"Right," said Lauren. "And we won't invite Ms. Becky and her gang."

"I can get her to show you some of the places where they do weightlessness training," I teased Lauren. "That'll cure your carsickness forever."

Lauren turned a little green just at the thought. "I'm only kidding," I promised her.

Lauren looked relieved.

The Oldest Fifth-Grader in History

I went back into the locker room in a considerably better mood than I had left it just an hour and a half before. Gymnastics does that for me sometimes. I can be in an absolutely lousy mood and think that nothing will change it, and then suddenly my spirits lift. That's really only happened since I've had Patrick as my coach.

"Colorado Springs, here we come," sang Lauren in the locker room. "Maybe one of the Olympic coaches will take a look at us, and say 'I want those girls on my team.'"

"It would have to be a coach for the Martian team," said Ashley.

"Why Martians?" asked Darlene. I would have

known not to feed Ashley a straight line. I can read people better than Darlene. Maybe it's because I've moved around a lot. Darlene can be too trusting. It's funny because she's moved around a lot also. Darlene doesn't have a mean bone in her body. Sometimes I feel like I have to protect her. She's older than me, but I'm much meaner than Darlene.

Ashley snickered. "Because only beings from outer space would want you on their Olympic team," she said.

"Maybe they have a special dormitory at the Olympic Center for kids from outer space," said Becky. "They can put all the Pinecones in there."

"Pinecones grow into mighty oaks," I said, trying to stick up for Darlene.

Becky hooted. "Oaks!" she cried. "Duh. . . ." She came over to me and rapped on my head with her knuckles. "Is anybody in there?" she asked.

I jumped away from her. "Becky, you are a royal pain."

"You're a real nut case," she said. "Pinecones grow into dum-dums, but real pinecones don't grow into oaks. They grow into what, class?"

"Evergreens," muttered Lauren.

"I knew that," I said. Talk about dumb. I mean, Patrick's club is called the Evergreen Academy.

There's an evergreen on our uniforms, for good ness' sake.

"So *that's* why Patrick calls us the Pinecones," said Cindi. "I never figured that out before." I gave her a grateful look. I knew she was only trying to take the heat off me, but unfortunately it only made me feel like more of a dunce head.

"Anyhow," said Lauren. "It's a proven fact that girls who go to the Olympic Center, go to the Olympics."

"That is the stupidest thing I've ever heard," said Ashley. "Thousands of girls go to the Olympic Center. Any tourist can go to the Olympic Center. I suppose all of them get on the Olympic team."

"Gotcha," said Lauren, playfully punching Ashley in the arm. "I didn't say that *all* girls who went to the Olympic Center went to the Olympics. But I bet every member of the Olympic team has also been to the Olympic Center."

Cindi laughed. "You'd better watch who you tangle with, Ashley," she said. "My friend Lauren, here, is always at the head of the class."

"Well, I'm in a *TAG* class."

"Are you sure that's not 'gag' class?" I asked.

"It's for Gifted and Talented, spelled backwards," said Ashley. "They do that so that the other kids don't get jealous. But of course, every-one knows what it means."

"I'd like to gift wrap her," muttered Darlene. "Will someone put that little shrimp back in a box?"

I laughed and started to get dressed. One thing about my friends — they don't mince words.

I opened my locker and threw my knapsack on the bench. I wrapped up my leotard into a ball. It would definitely need to go to the laundry. I remembered seeing a plastic bag in the waste-basket in the bathroom. I could use that to stick my leotard in and then it wouldn't mess up my schoolbooks. I went and got it.

"All right, who took it?" said Becky standing on a bench in the middle of the locker room.

I glanced down guiltily at the plastic bag in my hand. Only Becky could make you feel bad about taking a plastic bag out of the garbage.

"Sorry," I said. "I didn't know this was yours." I handed the bag to her.

"Very funny," she said, tossing it back to me. "Somebody took my permission slip for my par-ents from Patrick."

"I didn't take it," I said. I bent down to get the rest of my stuff from my locker.

"Wait a minute, there it is," said Becky. I didn't

pay any attention to her. If you tried to pay attention to everything that comes out of Becky's mouth, you'd be a lunatic.

Then I heard Becky's voice.

" 'Dear Ms. Sutton, I am sorry to inform you —' "

"Hey!" I shouted.

"That's never good news," said Gloria.

"I am sorry to inform you that once again I believe Jodi is having problems in school."

"That's private," I yelled. "That's none of your business!"

"Give that back to Jodi," hollered Lauren. She sounded furious.

"I will, I will," said Becky. "I just picked it up by mistake. I thought it was my permission slip."

"You are a total jerk, Becky; you know that, don't you?" said Lauren.

"*Moi*?" said Becky. "I'm the jerk? I don't get notes from my teacher telling me that I'm a chronic problem. If anyone has a case of terminal jerkdom, I'd say it's you Pinecones." She handed me back the note. "Sorry," she said. Just call her Ms. Insincerity.

I stuffed the note back into my knapsack.

Becky left the locker room. She even looked a little embarrassed. The other Pinecones moved very slowly as if they didn't want to leave me alone but didn't know what to say, either.

I shrugged my knapsack onto my shoulders.

"See ya," I mumbled.

"Hey, Jodi," shouted Darlene. "Becky's the real dumb one, not you."

"Yeah, really," I said. Unfortunately that was a total lie. Becky went to private school with Darlene, and I happened to know that she was in the honors class, just like precious Ashley. The only reason Lauren and Cindi weren't in a special class was that our school has an open plan, trying to integrate the 'gifted' with us regular folk. That was one reason why Mom liked the school and deliberately picked a town house in that district.

"Did Ms. Assante give you that note because you did a cartwheel in the hall?" Cindi asked. She turned to Darlene. "It was a good cartwheel. Some kid gave her a 9.9."

"Unfortunately he was in second grade," I said.

"I *liked* your miner's letter," said Lauren. Lauren has got to be about the most loyal kid in the world. "I thought it was really imaginative. Much better than Jeffrey's. Anybody can think of a baby dying in the snow."

"What do you study in that school?" asked Darlene.

"Writing," I groaned. "That's all we do. Write

all day long. Ms. Assante's a writing nut. I may repeat the fifth grade forever. I'll be the oldest fifth-grader in history."

"Don't be silly," said Cindi. "You're not that dumb."

I looked at her. "Not that dumb." Did Cindi really think I was dumb? Sure, I didn't get good grades like her, but did she think being funny was easy?

"Whoops," Cindi said. She was blushing. She knew she had hurt my feelings. "You know, I didn't mean it. I meant you weren't dumb at all."

"Forget it," I said. "Don't sweat it."

But I was hurting. I mean, if even your good friends think you're kind of dumb, what hope is there?

I Hate the Words "Wait and See"

Darlene was coming to our house for dinner that night. It would be the first time that she was ever at my house. I had been to her house for a party. I was a little embarrassed 'cause Darlene's older, but Darlene had sounded glad to come.

All the way home in the car, she had babbled about how excited she was about going to Colorado Springs. "Are you coming, Ms. Sutton?" Darlene asked.

Mom shook her head. "No, somebody's got to mind the store. We'll still be having classes. But I think it's a terrific opportunity for all of you. It'll give Jodi a chance to see her sister."

"Well, I can't wait," said Darlene. "As soon as I get home, I'm gonna start figuring out what to pack."

I laughed. I like Darlene. You'd think someone like her would act like going to the Olympic Center was no big deal. She gets to meet professional athletes and stars all the time.

I'm a little bit in awe of Darlene, not because of her dad, but maybe that's a part of it. They have an awful lot more money than we have. I'm mean, we're really talking rich here.

But basically I just respect Darlene. She always seems so together, and I don't mean just her outfits. She's good at school. She's good at gymnastics, and she's nice to almost everybody. She never seems to get in a bad mood. Now me, my moods swing the way I do on the uneven bars.

My room is tiny. We live in a little town house complex not too far from the Evergreen Mall. I think the whole two-bedroom apartment could fit in Darlene's rec room.

"This is neat!" exclaimed Darlene. "I've got to get one in my room."

I looked around my room trying to figure out what I could possibly have that Darlene would think was neat. Then I saw she was staring at the low beam that I have in my bedroom. It's the full length, sixteen feet, but it sits on the floor. It takes up practically the entire bedroom. I'm so used to it, I hardly notice it.

"That used to be in our basement when we had a real house in St. Louis," I explained.

"No wonder you're so good," said Darlene.

She took off her shoes and socks and did a split. She did a turn on the beam and wobbled.

"Your hips went forward," I said. "Try to move in one piece."

Darlene tried the turn again. This time she did it perfectly.

"Thanks," she said. "You'll make a good coach someday."

"Me!" I exclaimed. "You've got to be kidding. I'd be a lousy coach. Mom always has to take these certification tests." I flopped down on my bed and watched Darlene do another turn. Every time she lifted a leg forward to start her turn, she flung her hips out.

"You've gotta keep your hips back," I said. "If your hips are square, you'll move in one piece."

"You *sound* like a coach," said Darlene. "I never thought of getting a low beam in my house. I gotta get my dad to buy me one of these. Where did you get it?"

"My dad built it," I said. "There's a big place that sells gymnastics supplies in Denver. You can get one there. But I think it costs a couple of hundred dollars."

Darlene nodded. "I have definitely got to get myself one of these." I wondered what it would be like to be able to get anything you want, no matter what it cost.

"Hey, look at your trophies!" Darlene exclaimed. "Are these all yours?"

My bookcase was full of trophies. A lot of them were huge with little gymnasts on top.

"Those belong to my sister," I said. "She didn't have room for all of hers in her dorm room at college. She left half of them in St. Louis. Mom's are downstairs. Here's mine." I giggled. I picked up the smallest one. "I got this last year."

"It's bigger than anything I've got," said Darlene. Darlene looked around the room. There was a picture on my wall of my sister competing on the beam. Everybody loves that picture. Jennifer's doing a split on the beam. "Is that your sister?" Darlene asked.

I nodded.

"She's not as pretty as you," said Darlene.

My mouth dropped open. My sister's got a perfect gymnast's body. She's short and looks totally together. Everyone always comments on how incredibly intense my sister seems in that picture. She's got a long face like me, but she inherited my dad's more muscular, stocky build and dark looks. She's got brown hair. Sometimes people can hardly believe we're sisters.

I'm built like a long, tall glass of water. In fact, I don't know what I'm gonna do if I don't stop growing. Gymnastics is hard to do if you're tall.

I've got long, strawberry-blonde hair, and I'm tall for my age. I'm almost as tall as Darlene and she's older than me. I like to fool around with my hair. Darlene and I are alike in that way. Darlene is black, and sometimes she braids her hair with beautiful beads. Then other times she wears it loose.

Judges can be very picky about your hair when you compete. It has to be neat and off your face. The judges can take off a tenth of a point if you fiddle with your hair while you're competing.

"Do you really think I'm prettier than my sister?" I asked.

Darlene gave me a sly smile. "You know, we're both pretty," she said. "It's hard to admit it, isn't it? I'm glad I'm pretty."

I blushed. "Me, too," I said. I felt as if I were sharing a deep, dark secret. It's not cool to admit that you like your looks, but sometimes I catch a glimpse of myself in the mirror and I like what I see.

We both looked in the mirror and played with our hair. Then I frowned.

"What's wrong?" Darlene asked, taking my hair and piling it on top of my head. "I like it this way."

"Do you think what they say about dumb blondes is true?" I asked. I had never told anybody before, but that cliché has always bothered me.

"Are you kidding?" said Darlene. "No way. One thing my mom and dad taught me is to never believe stuff like that. I've had to put up with that stuff all my life."

"You mean, 'cause you're black?" I asked.

Darlene shook her head. "Not just that. But everybody thinks football players are dumb. My dad is the smartest man I know, and all his life, he said, people thought he was dumb because he was big."

"Well, I'm tall, dumb, and blonde," I said, giggling.

"Everyone's gonna be jealous of you when you get to be a teenager. Maybe you'll be a model. My mom was a model. She says she had to put up with a lot of people thinking she was stupid just because of her job."

I looked at the picture of my sister up on the wall. "My sister is really prettier in real life than she is in the picture," I said. "Wait till you meet her."

"I wonder if we sleep in a dormitory at the Olympic Center or what?" Darlene asked.

"I don't know, " I said. "I hope they put all the Pinecones together."

"Me, too," said Darlene. "But if we have to split up, do you want to be my roommate?"

"Great." Life really wasn't so bad when you had friends. Maybe Mom's idea about having Darlene over without the other kids wasn't such a bad idea, after all.

Sometimes my mom is pretty smart about things.

I thought about the note in my knapsack. I'd show it to Mom after dinner. I knew she'd help me figure out what to say to Ms. Assante.

After dinner, Darlene's mom came to pick her up. She was still beautiful. I thought about what Darlene had said about people thinking she was dumb just because she was a model.

I helped Mom clean up. I wanted Mom in as good a mood as possible before she signed my permission slip to go to the mini-camp.

I put on rubber gloves. My hands were still raw from when I ripped my callus. Hot water hurt it.

"Darlene's a nice girl," said Mom as we finished the dishes.

"She's great," I said. "She asked me to be her roommate at the mini-camp." I fished out Patrick's note. "I guess you've got to sign this," I said. "But you already know all about it."

Mom picked up a pen and started to sign the permission slip without really reading it. She had already read it in Patrick's office.

"Oh, by the way," I said, hoping to just slip it in casually. "I have a note from Ms. Assante, too."

Mom held the pen poised above Patrick's permission slip. "What about?" she asked.

I wanted to bite my tongue. Talk about dumb blondes. That was the dumbest move in the book. Why had I opened my mouth *before* she signed Patrick's note?

"Uh, nothing . . . " I stammered. "I'll show it to you after you sign that note about the mini-camp."

"Let me see it," Mom said, carefully folding up Patrick's note.

I handed Mom the note from Ms. Assante. Mom

put on her reading glasses. She just got them and she hates to wear them. I wished she wouldn't be able to read the note, but she did. I knew I was sunk. She frowned as she read. Then she sighed. A frown and a sigh together were very bad omens.

"Jodi, what have you been doing?" she asked.

"Nothing," I said, "I did a cartwheel in the hall, that's all."

"It doesn't sound like that's all. I thought you were doing so well at your new school and at Patrick's, but this sounds so familiar. Ms. Assante says that you lack focus."

"Doesn't she say anything about lack of discipline?" I asked. I tried to make a joke.

Mom was not in the mood for my humor. "Yes, indeed, she does talk about your lack of discipline. Jodi, I don't want this to plague you all your life. We have to get a handle on it."

"But Mom, if I can learn a back somie quicker than Lauren, I can't be that dumb."

Mom was reading the note for a second time. Another bad sign. "She says that she's particularly worried about your writing skills."

"Nothing wrong with *your* writing skills, Mom," I tried to joke. "Just sign Patrick's note, okay? Then we'll worry about Ms. Assante. Patrick's note is more important."

Just call me Motor-Mouth. I knew I shouldn't have said that. Whenever I'm really nervous I crack jokes, and then I get in deeper trouble. Now Mom looked really angry, and that wasn't what I had meant to happen at all.

Mom put both notes away. "You'll have to miss a day of school for the camp. I think I'll wait until after we talk to Ms. Assante before I decide to let you skip school for gymnastics."

"But Mom, that's so unfair! One doesn't have anything to do with the other."

"School is more important than gymnastics. I've always tried to teach you that."

Now, where had I heard that before?

"I don't want you growing up thinking you can get away with poor grades because you're a gymnast," said Mom.

I kicked the table leg under the table. "Mom, I'm not asking for the world. I just want to go to Colorado Springs and see Jennifer."

"We will wait and see until after I talk to Ms. Assante."

"But all Ms. Assante cares about is dead miners," I protested.

Mom stared at me.

"What do dead miners have to do with my life?" I muttered.

"Jodi!" said my mother sharply. "History is

very important. I told you I am not going to make any decision about the mini-camp until after I talk to Ms. Assante. You will have to wait and see."

I hate those words "wait and see."

6

Jodi and the Lack of Disciplines

I was a red corpuscle carrying oxygen to the lungs. It was a game we were playing in gym. It's supposed to teach us about the body, and it's fun. I won the race to the lungs. I shook hands with Bobby, the boy who I beat. Since I won, he had to play a bubble of carbon dioxide and get exhaled through the nose. The nose was being played by Lauren.

"What's wrong with your hand?" Bobby asked.

I looked down. I didn't realize that my callus had ripped open again and was bleeding slightly.

"That's disgusting," said Bobby. I slipped my hand behind my back. "Sorry," I mumbled.

"Come on," said Lauren. "The nose is waiting!"

"The red corpuscle is bleeding real blood," yelled Bobby.

The gym teacher, Ms. Gilmour, blew her whistle. "Jodi, what is going on?" she asked.

"Nothing," I said, hiding my hand behind my back. "It's nothing."

"Her hand looks like it belongs on Godzilla," said Bobby.

"It does not," I said. "It's just a callus that I ripped in gymnastics."

"Let me see," said Ms. Gilmour. She looked at my palm. I had wiped the blood away.

"She's got hands like a boy," said Bobby.

"You're right, a cowboy," I said. "And I'm proud of them." Cindi and Lauren laughed a lot louder than any of the other kids. Ms. Gilmour looked at the clock. "We're just about out of time, anyhow," she said. "School's dismissed in five minutes. Jodi, your red corpuscle was a little bit too realistic, but you were fast."

"It's not fair," said Bobby. "Those girls are Amazons. We shouldn't have to compete against them. It's like they're professional athletes, or something."

"Scared of a little red-blooded competition?" I said, waving my hand in front of him.

"Ohhh . . . " he shrieked like I really was something out of a horror movie.

Lauren grabbed my arm. "Enough," she said. "Come on, let's get dressed."

I followed her and the other kids into the locker room. "It seems so stupid to have to get out of gym clothes to get dressed for dismissal to get back into gym clothes to go to Patrick's," said Cindi. "I think I'll just keep my gym shorts and T-shirt on."

"They stink," said Lauren.

Cindi sniffed under her armpit. "Not too ripe," she said. "I got my mom to sign Patrick's permission slip. Remind me to give it to him."

Lauren rolled her eyes. "Do not let me forget mine," she said. "It's worth its weight in gold to me. I had to talk to my parents for one whole hour before they would sign. I pointed out to them that you two guys would be going, too, so I wouldn't be the only one missing school. They bought that argument."

I got dressed silently. I took off my shorts. "Why don't you keep yours on like me?" asked Cindi.

"I've got to meet my mom," I mumbled.

"We do, too," said Lauren. "We'll meet her at Patrick's."

I shook my head and sighed. "No, I've got to meet her here in school. Ms. Assante has requested a conference."

"Uh-oh," said Lauren.

"Thanks for the vote of confidence," I said, shutting my locker.

"I didn't mean it that way," said Lauren, sounding hurt. I knew I had snapped at her when it wasn't her fault.

"I'm sorry," I said. "You guys go ahead. I'll meet you later."

My mother was already upstairs with Ms. Assante. Mom was sitting in the front row. The desk was way too small for her. She looked all scrunched up and embarrassed, but she smiled at me.

"I just came back from gym," I said. "I was a little bit too realistic as a red corpuscle."

Mom looked confused.

"It's the new gym program," explained Ms. Assante. "We teach the way the body works by having the kids act out the blood stream. I'm sure Jodi is very good. She's very fast."

"Thank you," I said.

"It's not her athletic ability that I'm worried about," said Ms. Assante, switching gears faster than I would have wished. "I know Jodi's in terrific physical shape; it's her mental shape that worries me. I wanted you here, Jodi, because there's nothing I would say to your mom that I wouldn't say to you."

"You wrote about Jodi being a discipline problem," said my mom.

"No, no," said Ms. Assante quickly. "Jodi really isn't a discipline problem. She's a good kid. I like her. It's just that Jodi *lacks* discipline, particularly in her writing." I wanted to groan. Maybe I could start a rock group: Jodi and the Lack of Disciplines.

Mom nodded as if this were all new to her, as if we hadn't heard it almost every year since kindergarten.

"Writing's boring," I blurted out. "I just can't do it."

Ms. Assante sat up. I knew I shouldn't have said that writing was boring. She loved writing; she wanted us to experience the joy of creativity. What if you just aren't creative? It's no joy, believe me.

"Jodi," said Ms. Assante. "You can't find everything we write about boring."

"I do," I said.

"Jodi!" said my mother sharply. "You're being rude."

Ms. Assante held up her hand to interrupt my mother. It was almost as if for a second Ms. Assante was the student.

"No, I appreciate Jodi's honesty," said Ms. Assante. "Jodi, I challenge you to find something interesting to write about. It can be on any subject."

"It's not the subject," I protested. "It's me. Dumb kids can't write interesting."

"Jodi, you're not dumb," argued my mother.

"You don't see Lauren or Cindi here, do you?" I asked. "They aren't missing gymnastics because they have to stay late at school *two* days in a row."

"Some things may be more important than gymnastics," said Ms. Assante. "Look at this, Ms. Sutton."

Ms. Assante got out a sheaf of papers. "These are Jodi's reports from the last month. She spelled New York, *New Yorak*; auditorium, *autirorym*. I expect such errors from young students, but at Jodi's age, she has to learn to master this problem. It's not the spelling that bothers me. It's that Jodi seems to have given up on her writing."

"Is this true, Jodi?" asked my mother.

"I told you. I can't find anything interesting to write about."

"I have asked the children to keep a journal," said Ms. Assante. "Jodi refuses to cooperate."

"She is going to start cooperating," said my

mother determinedly. "Believe me, she is going to start. What do you want her to do? I will see that she does it."

Ms. Assante looked from my mother to me. "I would like Jodi to get used to feeling like a writer. I want her to write *two* pages in her journal *every* day."

"But the other kids only have to write one page," I argued.

"You had your chance to be like the other kids," said Ms. Assante. "You flunked it."

"How can anybody flunk something that we're not being graded on?" I cried.

Ms. Assante frowned at me. "You found a way," she said.

"But I'll never be able to write *two* pages a day," I said. "And do my other homework *and* do gymnastics."

"Then perhaps you'll have to cut back on gymnastics," said Ms. Assante. She glanced at my mother. "I'm sorry," she said. "I know how important gymnastics is to your family."

"Not more important than school," said my mother quickly.

"Thank you," said Ms. Assante softly. "But you and I agreeing doesn't help. We have to get Jodi to do the work."

I sat with my arms folded across my chest.

Mom turned to me. She put her hand gently on my forearm. "Jodi, you do see, don't you, that Ms. Assante just wants to help?"

"Great help," I muttered. "I couldn't do it before, so now I have to do twice as much as the other kids. That's not fair."

"It's not punishment," said Ms. Assante. "You can write on any subject you want," said Ms. Assante.

"I don't have anything to write about!"

"Jodi," snapped my mother. "We are not going to keep circling around this issue. You will do the writing. If, after two weeks, Ms. Assante thinks you genuinely have improved, and have kept up your end of the bargain by writing in your journal, you can go to Colorado Springs. If not, you can't."

"What is this about Colorado Springs?" asked Ms. Assante.

"There's a gymnastics mini-camp that Jodi's group has been invited to participate in," explained my mother. "She will not be going unless she completes her journal for you."

Ms. Assante closed my notebook. "Ordinarily I don't believe in bribing students."

"This isn't a bribe," said my mother. "I simply do not feel right about encouraging Jodi in gymnastics when she refuses to work at school."

Ms. Assante stood up and looked at her watch. "Unfortunately I have a faculty meeting. Jodi, do you understand what we decided on?"

"Yes," I grumbled. "You all just decided that I wasn't going to Colorado Springs. Thank you very much."

I gritted my teeth, fighting back the urge to cry. At least I had some pride, but it did seem so unfair. I'd never get to go to Colorado Springs. No matter how much I tried, Mom and Ms. Assante would say that I hadn't done enough, that I didn't believe school was important. Well, I didn't care about the stupid journal. I looked out the window at the mountains. Somewhere to the south, over the pass, was Colorado Springs. It was only an hour away, but it might as well have been on the moon.

7

Backwards, Backwards, Backwards

Mom drove me to Patrick's. I sat next to the car door, as far away from her as I could, and stared out the window.

"Neither Ms. Assante nor I want to punish you," said Mom.

"Right," I muttered. "It's for my own good." I hate those words "for your own good." They're almost as bad as "lack of discipline."

"It *is* for your own good," insisted my mother. "I want you to go to Colorado Springs. I think you'll have a terrific time."

"It's easy," I said, "Just let me go without making me write a whole book. I can't do it. Ms. Assante said she didn't believe in bribes."

"It's not a bribe, and nobody's asking you to write a book. It's just two pages a day in your journal," answered Mom. She turned into the road by the Evergreen Mall that led to the gym. "Think of it as fun."

Snow was beginning to melt in dirty piles by the cottonwood trees. Maybe I could write how lousy snow felt in the spring. How could Mom be so stupid and say, "think of it as fun"?

Mom parked the car and pulled her gym bag from the backseat. I followed her into Patrick's gym. I would be able to pick out Mom's walk in the middle of a million people. She walks like a champion. Her weight is on the balls of her feet, with her shoulders squared back.

I squared my shoulders, too, but I didn't feel like a champion.

We worked on the vault at the beginning of practice. I was glad. I like the vault because it happens so fast. Darlene hates the vault. She doesn't like throwing herself at an immovable object headfirst.

Now me, I love it. One split second and zoom, you either nail it or you don't.

I started my run, keeping my elbows close to my body, and pumping them up and down for maximum speed the way I had as a red corpuscle. I looked straight ahead so that I could see the horse and the board at the same time. Patrick has taught us to run on the balls of our feet, not on our tippy toes.

I did a straddle vault. Patrick grabbed my arms and guided me down as I snapped my legs together.

"Great!" he said. "Almost picture perfect. Do you know what you did right that time?"

I was breathing hard. "I leaned backwards on my jump so I got more height from the run."

Patrick clapped me on the back like I was a grade-A student.

It was Cindi's turn to vault next.

"But I don't really get it," she said. "It happens so fast I don't have time to think. My brain doesn't keep up with my body."

"Your brain is doing just fine," said Patrick. "Use it."

Cindi didn't reach for the horse soon enough. It's funny how you can see somebody else make a mistake. She didn't have enough height, so she didn't have a chance to open her legs and do a really good straddle.

She sort of collapsed on the crash mat in a heap. "How many points do I get for crash-landing?" Cindi asked.

Patrick laughed and helped her up. "None," he said. "Let's work on tumbling before everybody's exhausted. I've been asked to demonstrate my spotting techniques on the floor exercises. I want to show them that it's not brute strength that counts, but knowing what your student can do. You don't need brute strength if the gymnast is ready."

"I don't know, Patrick," said Lauren. "You're pretty strong. I wouldn't want a little shrimp spotting me."

"You are a little shrimp," Becky reminded her.

"I know exactly what Patrick is talking about," said Ashley. "Jodi's mother isn't huge, but she's a great spotter. When she's spotting me, I can feel the movement."

"Thank you, Ashley," said Patrick. "That's exactly what I want to show them at the mini-camp. Let's practice some of our tumbling runs."

We did a forward roll into two front hand-springs.

I didn't even need Patrick's spot for my second handspring. He gave me an approving nod.

"Jodi," said Patrick after the other girls had finished their tumbling passes. "I want to work on your back somersault again. Are you ready?"

"When is Jodi ever *not* ready to try something new?" joked Darlene.

I'll admit I've got a reputation for being a little reckless. "Let me at it," I said.

Patrick grinned at me. "Okay, try it." I stood up, ready to start. Patrick had his hand on my back. I sprang up, and just the light twist of Patrick's hand reminded me when to tuck. I got around, but I really didn't have enough height. I collapsed in a heap on the mat because I didn't have enough time to open up.

"Let me try again," I said. I could see that the back somersault was very different from a back handspring. You need much more height.

"She's just a glutton for punishment," said Ashley. "Can't I try it next?"

"I want Jodi to do it one more time to get the feel of it. I was thinking of using Jodi in my demonstration." Patrick looked at me. "If that's all right with you," he said.

I kept my eyes on the blue mat. I wanted to scream and fling myself on the blue mat like a baby having a temper tantrum. Patrick wanted to use *me*, and I couldn't go. I was being kept behind because of a stupid journal that I'd *never, never* be able to write.

"You'd better try it with Ashley," I said to Patrick, clipping off the ends of my words. "I'm not going to the mini-camp."

"Goody," said Ashley, jumping up. "I'm littler, so it will be easier, won't it Patrick?"

"Wait a minute," said Patrick. "What do you mean, you're not going?"

"I'm *not* going," I said. Something inside me just snapped. I ran out of the gym, something I had never done to Patrick. I just had to get out of there, or everybody would see me cry.

8

The Return of the Pinecones

I almost never cry. It's just not my nature, so when the tears came bubbling out on the gym floor, I couldn't take it. Usually I can keep tears away with a wisecrack, but when Patrick mentioned wanting to use *me* to demonstrate his coaching techniques, I wanted to scream.

I tore into the locker room. I slammed my palm into the wall next to the locker. I knew I had to go back out on the floor. It's very bad discipline to leave the gym floor, and I didn't want Patrick to be mad at me. Everything was such a mess.

I wiped my eyes and started back out. I'm a lot of things, but I'm not a quitter. I hated the idea of that little Miss Perfect Ashley taking my place.

She might have to take my place at the mini-camp, but I was still a gymnast.

I pushed on the swinging door of the locker room. It pushed back. Lauren, Cindi, and Darlene charged in, practically knocking me on the floor.

"We've come to make you go back out there," said Lauren. "I can't take Ashley bragging about taking your place."

I rubbed my head where I had hit myself on the swinging door. "I was on my way back out," I said. "You don't have to panic."

"We weren't panicking," said Darlene. "But you looked totally unglued out there. Are you okay? You looked like you were crying. Even when you rip on bars, I've never seen you cry."

"We go to school with her," said Cindi. "And we've never seen her cry."

"Is Patrick mad at me?" I asked.

Cindi sat down on the bench. "Not at all," she said. "We asked permission to come talk to you, and he thought it was a good idea. What got you so upset?"

Cindi sounded so concerned it made me want to cry again. I was driving myself nuts with suddenly turning into a faucet. I wiped my eyes with the sleeve of my leotard.

"Here," said Darlene, going into the bathroom

and coming out with a whole roll of toilet paper. "You look like you need this."

"I hope I don't need all of this, " I said, giggling through my tears. "This is rough," I started to sniff again. "This is embarrassing." I started to cry again. "I'm sorry."

"Don't be sorry," said Lauren. "Just tell us what's gone wrong. We're your friends."

I sniffed. "It's my mom. She and Ms. Assante. They won't let me go to Colorado Springs. Ms. Assante says I'm too stupid, and I shouldn't miss school. My mom agrees with her."

"What!" exclaimed Darlene, practically hitting the ceiling. "That's so unfair!"

"That's what I think," I said. "Who cares what I do in school? It's got nothing to do with going on this trip. But that's the deal. I can't go. And then when I found out that Patrick wanted to use me to demonstrate what a good coach he was, I just fell apart."

"I'm going out there and give your mom a piece of my mind," said Darlene. "It is just totally unjust."

"Uhh, wait a minute," I said, hesitating. I put my hand on Darlene's shoulder. "Not so fast. It might not be a good idea. Mom's in a really foul mood." I really didn't want Darlene going out and embarrassing Mom in front of Patrick, especially when I hadn't exactly told the whole story.

"It stinks to call you dumb," said Cindi. "Your mom's a gymnast. She must see how smart you are here."

"Well," I admitted, "it wasn't exactly Mom who said I was dumb. It was Ms. Assante."

"Who's Ms. Assante?" said Darlene. "I'll go tell *her* off. Where is she?"

"She's our teacher," said Lauren. "But that doesn't sound like her. She wouldn't call Jodi dumb. I don't get it. Why won't your mom let you go to the mini-camp? Does it have to do with that note from Ms. Assante?"

"Exactly," I said, warming up to the subject. "They cooked it up between themselves. It is totally unfair. Totally!"

Lauren frowned. "Run it by me again."

"What?" I asked.

"Why can't you go to the mini-camp?" asked Lauren. "It doesn't make sense. I can't see your mom *or* Ms. Assante calling you dumb and saying because you're dumb you can't go. Your mom isn't like that."

"Well, they might just as well have said it," I argued. "Ms. Assante says my writing needs work. Unless I write *two* pages in the journal *every* day, I can't go to the mini-camp."

Darlene paced in circles. "Say what?" she asked. "What's this about a journal?"

"Our teacher makes us keep a journal," Cindi explained. "We don't get graded on it, but we have to write in it every day."

"Let me get this straight," said Lauren. "It's not that you can't go, but that you don't want to go."

"What do you mean, *I* don't want to go?"

"Well, it seems to me that if you keep a journal and do the work, then you can go."

"I have to write twice as much as you do. I'll never be able to do it." I was getting angry all over again.

"It's just two pages a day. That's not so much."

"That's easy for you to say. Everything comes easy to you."

"Oh, sure," said Lauren. "It takes me forever to figure out how to do even a simple back handspring, and Patrick shows you a back somersault once, and you've got it."

"Lauren's got a point," said Cindi. "You do pick up the moves faster than anyone else."

"Write about gymnastics," said Darlene.

"My teacher doesn't know anything about gymnastics," I argued.

"All the better," said Darlene. "She won't know

what you're talking about. You can fill up two pages easily just talking about flip-flops, and Valdezes. She'll think you're speaking a foreign language."

"You really think I can do it?" I asked.

"What's your alternative? Letting that little twerp Ashley take your place in Colorado Springs?" said Lauren.

I paused. "That's no alternative . . . that's a disaster," I said.

We walked out together to the gym. Patrick glanced up at us. "The return of the Pinecones," he said.

"It's more like the return of the living dead," said Becky under her breath.

Patrick finished working with Becky's group. He had us do some conditioning. When we had finished our push-ups, I asked if I could talk to him alone for a minute.

"I'm sorry I ran out like that," I said to Patrick.

"I'm glad you apologized," said Patrick. "It's not the kind of behavior I expect from you. Is it anything you want to talk to me about?"

Patrick was so much easier to talk to than all my teachers at school. But still I didn't trust myself to talk to him about this. I shook my head. "No . . . just something from school that was upsetting me. But if you still want me, and Mom lets me go, I'd be honored to be the one who does the demonstration with you."

"You were always my first choice," said Patrick.

I grinned at him. Patrick could make me feel like a milllion dollars. Ms. Assante made me feel like a penny.

9

Writer's Block
for Blockheads

It sounded so easy: write two pages a day and I'd get to go to Colorado Springs. I sat down at my desk after dinner, sure that it would be a cinch. I sharpened my pencil. Isn't that what writers are supposed to do?

Then I decided it would be better if I wrote in pen. I put a pen and pencil in front of me. Then I couldn't choose. I opened the journal, and tried to decide whether pencil or pen would be better.

I felt thirsty. I went into the kitchen for a glass of water. Mom was washing the dishes.

"Do you need help?" I asked, grabbing a dish towel.

"How's your journal coming?" Mom asked.

"Fine," I lied. I picked up a plate. I was in bad shape if I'd rather dry dishes than go upstairs to my room and write.

"Mom, did you know that Patrick has to give a coaching demonstration in Colorado Springs?" I asked.

Mom laughed. "Are you kidding? He's as nervous about that as a kid having to give an oral report. Not that I blame him. A lot of people who coached him in college and high school will be there."

I coughed. "Did you know he has to pick a kid to do the demonstration with?"

Mom looked me straight in the eye. "And who does he want?" she asked, smiling.

"Me," I said.

"Actually he did tell me. I told him that it depended on you. I didn't tell him why. I thought that was private between you, me, and Ms. Assante."

"But Mom, it would be such an honor! Don't you want me to be the one he uses in his demonstration?" I put the last dish away and looked around the kitchen for anything else to clean up. I picked up a glass.

"That's not dirty," said Mom, putting it back down.

"You sure?" I asked holding it up to the light

the way they do in the TV ads. "I think I see dishwasher spots."

Mom took the glass from my hand. "Young lady, I have the feeling that if you want to go to Colorado Springs you'd better march back to your room, and get to work."

"Yes, ma'am," I said.

I went back to my room. I circled the beam on the floor. I took off my socks and shoes and walked across the beam on my tiptoes. Maybe I'd be inspired if I did a somersault. I did a forward roll on the beam, but I put my head down too fast and I fell off.

Mom heard the thud and knocked on my door. "Jodi?" she asked. "Are you all right?"

"I was just writing an explanation point!" I said.

Mom opened the door. She saw me sprawled on the floor by the beam.

"Jodi," she said. She pointed a finger at my desk. I got up and sat down at my desk chair.

"Close the door Mom. I need privacy," I said over my shoulder.

Mom closed the door. I chewed on the pencil. I had almost gnawed through to the lead when the phone rang.

Mom called up to me. "Jodi, it's for you. Don't talk long," she warned.

It was Cindi. "So, how much have you written?" Cindi asked.

I groaned. "You're as bad as my mom," I whispered into the mouthpiece.

Cindi giggled. "Sorry, but I just finished writing my page and I thought I'd call to encourage you. If that twerp Ashley does the demonstration instead of you, it'll kill me."

"It'll kill me more. She really is a Becky-in-training," I said.

"Becky-in-Training. That's a good name for her. She's a bit much," said Cindi.

"She's a B.I.T.," I said.

Cindi laughed. "It can be our secret name for her, 'Little Bit.' "

"I like it, I like it," I said.

Mom was giving me one of her patented get-off-the-phone-and-back-to-work looks.

"I got to go, Cindi," I said.

I hung up. Mom pointed to my room. "I'm going, I'm going," I said. "A house is not supposed to be a jail."

"I know," said Mom. "I'd just like you to get your work done."

"I've already written over a page," I lied.

"Great," said Mom.

I went back up to my room and did a split on my low beam and looked up at my journal. I wasn't any more inspired.

I got up and sat down with my chewed-up pencil. Then I picked up the pen. I chewed on the pen top. At least I wouldn't get lead poisoning.

About twenty minutes later, with the same blank, lined page staring at me, the phone rang again.

"Jodi!" Mom yelled.

It was Lauren. "How's it going?" she asked.

"What is this, the Pinecone Homework Brigade?" I asked.

"Why?" asked Lauren. "Who else called?"

"Cindi."

Lauren laughed. "Oh, yeah, she told me about the new nickname for Ashley."

"Too bad I can't put that in my journal," I said.

"Well," said Lauren. "Ms. Assante does say she wants you to be as honest as possible."

"Yeah, well I've already finished today's part," I lied.

"Great," said Lauren.

I hung up and went back to my room. It was definitely not a good sign that I was lying to my friends as well as to my mother about the stupid journal.

I slammed it shut. I hated the thing. Ms. Assante would open it up and find all blank pages. She'd tell my mom that I hadn't kept my part of the bargain, and I'd never get to go.

I paced up and down on my beam. Why couldn't I just do gymnastics and forget about school? I wondered if I could run away and join the circus. I could go to St. Louis and visit my dad, but he cared about school even more than Mom.

The phone rang. It was Darlene. "So?" she asked.

"You're the last of the Pinecone Brigade to call in," I said. "You're all checking up on me."

"It's only 'cause we care," said Darlene.

"I know," I admitted.

"We don't want the little twerp to get her chance because you couldn't write two lousy pages."

"Did you hear my new name for Ashley? 'Becky-in-Training'?"

Darlene laughed. "So, *did* you finish it?"

"No," I admitted. Maybe because Darlene didn't go to our school, I found it easier to tell the truth to her.

"Well, do it!" said Darlene.

"I was thinking about running away and joining the circus," I said. "I could be a cartwheeling clown."

"Running away and joining the circus is such a cliché," said Darlene. "It only happens in books. Just go write."

"Okay," I said.

But it wasn't okay. I went back into my room. My stomach was all clenched up in knots the way it is on days when I compete. I lay on my back on my bed and looked up at the picture of my sister on the wall.

I rolled over on my stomach. I had as much chance of seeing her in Colorado Springs with my friends as I had of flying to the moon. Only smart people get to fly to the moon.

I sat up and slammed the stupid journal shut for the last time. I'd just have to tell Ms. Assante that I got writer's block. Can you get writer's block if you've never written anything? Maybe there's a writer's block for blockheads.

The Coach's Pet

I took my journal with me to gymnastics class. It was still blank. I had tried and tried, but I couldn't do it. I couldn't think of anything to say. I had to write something. Time was running out. I only had a week left. I took it out of my knapsack and dug into my pocket for a pen.

Becky walked by me. She walks up on her toes. She turned toward me and gave me a dirty look. I'm not sure Becky has any nice looks. She looked like a buzzard in a zoo. I'm sure she thought she looked like a swan, but if you've ever seen a buzzard in the zoo, their necks kind of swivel. It reminded me of Becky. Becky hates to think she's missing anything. She always checks out who Patrick is working with and who he thinks is good.

Suddenly I thought about how much Ms. Assante likes us to use animals to describe people. I opened my journal and wrote.

She moves across the room like a buzzard in a leotard, walking on tiptoes instead of claws —

"What are you writing?" Becky asked me. I closed my notebook firmly. "Uh, nothing," I stammered. I could feel my cheeks turning red. But she *had* looked like a buzzard on tiptoe.

"You were looking at me and writing," said Becky.

"It's just schoolwork," I said.

"You're not supposed to do homework during gymnastics," said Becky.

"I had a free moment," I said.

Patrick signaled me. I made sure that I zipped the notebook into my knapsack.

Becky walked over to Patrick. She walked with her toes turned out like a ballerina, or a buzzard. She pointed to me.

"It's not fair," said Becky. "Just because Jodi's mom works here, she thinks she gets special privileges. She brought her homework into the gymnasium."

Patrick sighed. "I don't like tattletales," he said to Becky. "You worry about yourself. I'll worry about Jodi."

It was my turn to work on my floor routine. I started with my handstand pirouette. A pirouette is a turn, and you actually "dance" on your hands. It takes a lot of upper body strength. I never quite made it around the 360 degrees.

But since I've been working with Patrick, I've really gotten stronger. I could actually feel myself get stronger from week to week because of working on handstands.

"Okay," said Patrick. "Let's work on your tumbling run again. I want to show how you use the momentum from the roundoff to a back handspring series to a tucked back somersault."

"Whew, I'm not sure I can say all that, much less do it," I said.

"Let's try it."

I stood with my hands on my hips trying to visualize stringing those movements together. The tricks by themselves weren't that hard, except for the somie. We had been really working on that, and I knew Patrick would spot me for it. I didn't have to do it on my own. Still, it's putting all the movements together into a tumbling pass that takes all your energy.

I started my run, but I was off-center, and I didn't have enough power to do the second handspring, much less the somersault without Patrick literally shoveling me up and around. I could hear him grunt with the effort of spotting me.

"Sorry," I said.

"On that one I *did* need brute strength," said Patrick. "Do you know what you did wrong?" That's Patrick's favorite question.

I shook my head. "It just felt off, right from the roundoff."

"You've got to start leaning back from the snap through," said Patrick. "Let me show you."

Patrick did the sequence. He got incredible height from each move. I noticed that he wasn't going for horizontal distance, but for the height.

Lauren, Cindi, and Darlene applauded. "You trying to tell me that I'm gonna be doing that someday?" I said to Patrick.

"You can almost do it now," said Patrick.

He worked with the others on their tumbling runs while I watched intensely, trying to figure out what I was doing wrong.

I got out my notebook and started to write down the sequence. Ms. Assante had said we could write about anything we wanted. Lauren and Cindi had said to write about gymnastics. I wrote about putting together the back somie with the roundoff handspring. The more complicated gymnastics terms I used, the more Ms. Assante might be impressed.

Patrick called my name. "Jodi," he said. He sounded a little annoyed. "Jodi, you *aren't* supposed to work on homework during gymnastics. Becky is right about that."

"I'm writing about gymnastics," I explained to Patrick.

"Oh?"

"I was writing down the sequence you just taught me," I said. "I'm trying to write about how I'm learning to do a back somie. It's easier to do than to write."

"Come into my office later," said Patrick. "I've got some books that might help."

Patrick called Ashley and Becky's group to come work on their tumbling passes.

We Pinecones got to take a break. "Guess who's becoming the coach's pet?" asked Lauren.

"Ashley," I answered, as I watched Patrick work with her. I had to admit she was good.

Lauren poked me in the ribs. "Not her, silly. You."

"Me?"

" 'Me?' she says innocently," said Darlene. "Patrick has chosen her to show off in front of everybody at the mini-camp, and Jodi still acts surprised."

I stared at her. "Patrick tells you to come into his office later. He really likes you," said Cindi.

"I've never been anybody's pet," I said. I wondered if Cindi and Lauren were jealous.

Lauren laughed at me. "Knock, knock," she said, rapping me on the head.

"Who's there?" I asked.

"Patsy," said Lauren.

"Patsy who?" I knew I was destined to be Lauren's straight guy forever. I never got Lauren's jokes until the last minute.

Lauren patted me on the head. "Patsy dog on the head. She likes it."

I laughed a little nervously. "I always hate the teachers' pets. You guys don't hate me, do you?"

"Don't worry," said Cindi. "You still get in enough trouble in school. We're still your friends."

"Yeah," agreed Lauren. "Besides, someday you'll teach me to do a back somie."

I grinned. Patrick finished for the day. I waited for him. Mom came over to me. "Is anything wrong?" she asked.

I wondered why she always asked that first. Maybe because I was in trouble so much. Well, I'd show her. She was in for a big surprise. I smiled a little, thinking about being a coach's pet. I could live with that.

Patrick and Me:
Two of a Kind

I followed Patrick into his office. He pulled out a book with a dull brown cover. *The Biomechanics of Women's Gymnastics* by Gerald S. George.

He handed it to me. It had tiny print with a few little stick-figure drawings in it.

I looked at a stick figure doing a somie. I could see the difference between the one doing it the right way and the one doing it the wrong way, but when I tried to read it was like gobbledygook. "Inadequate flexibility and muscular control about the hip joints are generally the factors. . . ."

I put it down. Not only were the words too hard for me, I couldn't put them together in my brain.

"I'm too stupid to read this," I said.

"It's one of the best books I've got for breaking down movement," said Patrick.

"Trying to read it will give me a breakdown," I said.

Patrick laughed, something that I knew Ms. Assante wouldn't have done. I stared at the pictures some more. I showed Patrick the figure in the roundoff. "See, when I did my handspring, my legs were bent back like this figure, and so I couldn't get the snap."

"That's exactly it," said Patrick.

"But I can't write about it," I said.

"It's important that you 'see' what you're doing wrong," said Patrick. "That's what makes you so easy to teach."

I almost dropped to the floor. "I wish you'd tell that to my real teacher. She thinks I'm a dummy." I tried to make sense of the book again. "I'll never be able to write about this," I grumbled.

"Jodi, I don't get it. I'm glad you're trying to take notes about our work here, but why are you in such a sweat over writing about it?"

"Mom hasn't told you?" I asked.

"Told me what?"

I sighed. "The only way I can go to the mini-camp is if my teacher agrees that I've been keeping my journal."

"What do you mean?" Patrick asked.

I told him about the deal I had made with my mom and Ms. Assante about the journal.

"Your mother didn't tell me about it," said Patrick. "She did say that she didn't know if you could go. But she's been proud of you lately."

I blushed. It was strange to think of Mom and Patrick talking about me, stranger still to have Mom saying she was proud of me. I guess I had fooled her with all the time I had spent in my room, pretending to write.

"Mom, proud of me? That seems as weird as being the teacher's pet," I said. "I should write that down." I wrote it in my notebook.

Patrick put his feet up on his desk. "You're left-handed like me," he said. "Did you know that people used to think lefties were real oddballs?"

"I think they still do," I said.

"Naw. It's got definite advantages in gymnastics," said Patrick. "Left-handed people generally see things 'spatially.' They're often good at math and art. We just learn differently from other people. But it's got nothing to do with smart or dumb."

"Yeah, well, I *am* dumb, except in gymnastics.

I get by by making jokes," I admitted. "But lots of times I just don't understand stuff when I read it."

"Try to figure it out," said Patrick.

I groaned. "You gonna tell me to just try harder at school? That's what all adults say."

"I used to try to cover up that I felt dumb in school by making wisecracks," said Patrick. He took the book from me and stared at it himself.

"Like me," I said.

Patrick closed the book. "Have you noticed that you don't do it here, much? In fact, Lauren and Cindi are more likely to crack jokes. It's because they're less sure that they get it. People like you and me relax once we know we're on our own turf. We're just left-handed, right-brained odd-balls."

I kept hearing Patrick's words, "People like you and me."

"Did you get bad grades when you were a kid?" I asked.

"I repeated third grade," said Patrick. "I can still remember how humiliated I felt. But it was probably the best thing for me. I was having trouble learning to read. I wasn't even like you. I didn't get into gymnastics until I was in junior high, so when I was your age I thought I'd never be good at anything except flying paper airplanes and getting into trouble. Then I won a contest for the best designed airplane. That was the first time I didn't feel dumb."

"I can't believe that you felt like me," I said.

Patrick laughed. "I was a lot more like you than you think," he said. Patrick stood up. "I've got to go. You can stay and study these books if you'd like."

I was alone in Patrick's office. I took out my notebook and wrote the words "I'm not dumb. I just see things differently. I'm like Patrick. Patrick knows what it's like to feel stupid. But I watch Patrick work and teach me, and I *know* how smart he is. I'm not stupid."

Then I closed my notebook. I had written two and a half pages and the day wasn't even over yet. I was making up for lost time.

Make Way for Us,
Please

Ms. Assante stopped me as I was leaving school. "Tomorrow is the date you'll show me the journal, right?"

"Would I forget?" I said. I smiled. "I think you're going to be surprised." Man, I know I was. Ever since that day in Patrick's office, I had been writing up a storm. Some days I even filled three pages. I figured there was no way she wasn't going to be impressed.

"Pleasantly surprised?" Ms. Assante asked.

"Well, let me put it this way," I said. "For a right-brained kid, I don't think it's so bad."

"Right-brained?" echoed Ms. Assante. "What's that all about?"

"You'll read all about it tomorrow," I said. "I want to look it over tonight."

Ms. Assante smiled at me. "You sound like you're proud of it," she said. "I'm looking forward to reading it."

I joined Lauren and Cindi outside of class. "What was that all about?" Lauren asked. "Have you handed in your journal?"

"Tomorrow," I sang. I sang the song from *Annie* that we have to do in chorus.

"Jodi's in a good mood," said Cindi. "Watch out for her in gymnastics. She'll be a terror."

"Some days I wrote more than two pages. Mom's got to let me go with you guys to Colorado Springs."

"I'd like to read it," said Lauren.

I giggled. "I did write some descriptions of Becky that are pretty funny."

"Ms. Assante may have created a monster," said Cindi. "Next thing you know you'll be writing funny things about us."

I shook my head. "No way. You guys have been real loyal friends."

"Really loyal," corrected Lauren. "Want me to check your grammar and spelling?"

I patted my journal. "Nope, it's sort of too personal. But I really didn't mind doing it as much as I thought."

"I like writing in my journal," said Cindi. "It's the only place I get real privacy." Cindi comes from a big family. She's got four older brothers. Sometimes her house feels like you're in a TV sitcom. Her brothers all play football. They're big and make a lot of noise.

"Did you write about your brothers?" I asked.

"I wrote about what life would be like without them," said Cindi. "I started a science-fiction fantasy where my brothers got shrunk to the size of a pinhead."

"I wrote about what it would be like to be as good as Ashley," said Lauren. "I'm so jealous of her. She's only nine years old, and it kills me that she can do a perfect somie and I can't."

"You'll get it," I said. "You just have to use the right side of your brain more."

"Excuse me?" said Lauren.

"You just need more practice using the right side of your brain, the way I needed practice writing."

"Thank you, Professor," said Lauren.

"Come on," said Cindi. "We'll be late for gymnastics." We caught the bus to the Evergreen Mall. I pulled out my journal and started to look it over. There were about a hundred spelling mistakes. Maybe I should let Lauren check it over, I thought.

Cindi pulled the buzzer for our stop. We walked up the side road to the gym. The snow was definitely melting, and the sun was still high in the sky even at three-thirty in the afternoon. Spring. My favorite time of year. Maybe I would make my last journal entry be about spring.

A car honked at us. It was Darlene's mom giving Becky and Darlene a ride. They waited for us at the entrance.

"I was just asking Darlene what she was planning on taking to the mini-camp," said Becky.

Becky had a different leotard for every day of the month, but then, so did Darlene. If those two ever had a fashion contest, they'd leave the rest of us far behind.

The difference was that Darlene was nice and Becky was a snob. It's amazing how something will bother you in someone you don't like, but it just seems funny in someone you like. Friends were the best thing in the world. Maybe I'd have to write that in my journal, too.

"Knock, knock," said Darlene.

"Who's there?" I asked.

"That was my question," said Darlene. "You don't look like you are here. Are you coming?"

I followed them into the locker room. I took out my journal to write down my thought about friendship. "A friend is like putting ice on a bruise. Ice is cold, but a friend heals. A friend's jokes never wound." I stared down at what I had written. It was a poem, or at least I thought it was a poem. I thought it was beautiful. I read it again.

"Knock, knock," said Lauren.

I looked up, startled. I really had been in another world. "Huh?" I said. I blushed and closed my notebook. "Sorry."

"I just realized that I know a gymnastics knock-knock joke," said Lauren. "Want to hear it? Knock, knock."

"Who's there?" asked Cindi.

"Olga," said Lauren.

"Olga who?" I asked.

"Olga home if you don't let me in."

"I don't get it," said Ashley. "Why is that a gymnastics joke?"

"You've never hear of Olga Korbut?" said Darlene. "You *are* a baby."

"I am not," said Ashley, but she stuck out her lower lip and she looked, well, to be honest, she looked nine years old. "I've got a knock-knock joke for you," said Ashley. "Knock, knock."

"Who's there?" asked Darlene warily.

"Pecan," said Ashley.

"Pecan who?"

"Pecan somebody your own size," said Ashley.

She laughed hard. Darlene didn't seem to think it was very funny. Ashley went out into the gym. "That little peanut gets me," said Darlene.

"Our own B.I.T."

"I just wish she wasn't so good," said Lauren.

"Wait a minute," I said. "Do I detect that some of us Pinecones are turning a little green?"

"Is that gonna lead in to another dumb knock-knock joke?" asked Darlene, putting her hands on her hips.

"No . . . it's just that we all sound jealous. It's not Ashley's fault she's good. It's Ashley's fault she's a pill. She's hard to swallow. But remember. She may be a pill, but we're not going to let her get to us."

"Yes, unfortunately, she's better than we are," said Darlene.

"Yeah, but she's not more fun. Who is going to have the most fun at this mini-camp?" I asked.

"The Pinecones," said Darlene, Cindi, and Lauren together.

I started singing a song. *"We are the Pinecones . . . We fall from trees . . . We have skinned knees . . . Make way for us, please. . . ."* I paused and wrote it in my journal. I could see Ashley staring at us from across the locker room.

I put my journal back into my knapsack and

zipped it closed. I repeated the song I had just made up. Lauren, Becky, and Darlene picked up the refrain.

We waltzed out of the locker room with our arms linked, singing, *"We are the Pinecones. We fall from trees. We have skinned knees. Make way for us, please. . . ."*

Becky and Gloria were doing their warm-ups. We sang our song to them. "That is the stupidest song I have ever heard," said Becky. "Jodi's a poet, and don't I know it. Her feet are like Long-fellow's and they sure show it."

"And smell it," added Gloria.

Ashley had followed us out of the locker room. She snickered. The truth of the matter is that I do have long feet.

Patrick clapped his hands. "I like the fact that the Pinecones have a theme song," he said.

"We'll sing it again," I shouted. When we got to the chorus, *"MAKE WAY FOR US, PLEASE,"* we pushed past Becky's group and each did a cartwheel onto the end of the floor mats.

Patrick and a few of the other girls applauded.

"Amateur," muttered Becky.

"I liked it," said Patrick.

I had a great day after that. We started with the tumbling. I remembered the stick figures in

Patrick's book. As I finished the roundoff, I leaned backwards into my handspring, and I had plenty of momentum left over for my somie.

I only needed Patrick's help in the last part of my tuck coming out of the somie. It was the best I had ever done it. Patrick lowered me down.

"You've almost got it!" he exclaimed. "I'd like to do it just that way for the demonstration."

Mom had paused to watch me. She gave me a thumbs-up sign. "If I go," I said, swallowing the words. Just seeing Mom reminded me that everything depended on whether or not Ms. Assante thought my journal was good enough.

But still I felt pretty good. I hadn't copped out the way I sometimes did on schoolwork. I had tried my hardest. Tomorrow I'd find out whether it was good enough.

I sank down on the mat and turned to watch the other Pinecones do their tumbling runs. Tomorrow would come soon enough. I was a lot more scared than I realized. What if my journal wasn't any good? What if Ms. Assante thought it was stupid? I sighed. There was nothing more I could do now.

13

A Pile of Nothing

At the end of class, Patrick said he wanted to talk to me. The rest of the kids went into the locker room. Ashley stopped next to us.

"Did you want to see me?" she asked Patrick.

"No, Ashley," he said. "You had a good workout today. I wanted to talk to Jodi about the demonstration at the mini-camp."

Ashley flung me a dirty look.

"She thinks you should have picked her," I said.

"I wanted to go over what we'll do in Colorado Springs," said Patrick, ignoring my comment about Ashley.

"I won't know if I can go until tomorrow or the

next day," I told Patrick. "After Ms. Assante reads my journal. I have to hand it in tomorrow."

"Would you rather I wait until then to talk to you about it?" Patrick asked.

I nodded. I really was nervous. I felt it might jinx my luck if I planned on being able to go.

Patrick put his hand on my back. "Okay," he said. "After you find out if you can go, we'll talk. Good luck tomorrow."

I sighed. I opened the swinging door to the locker room and then I froze. I heard my words coming out of a high, squeaky voice. "She moves across the room like a buzzard in a leotard . . . on tiptoes instead of claws."

My mind raced so fast. I knew immediately that somebody had found my journal and that my life had just taken one mighty nosedive into disaster.

"Who do *you* think she's writing about?" Becky's voice sounded shrill. "I know it was me."

I tore into the room. Ashley was holding my notebook up to her nose. "I'm not dumb," she read, her voice rising hysterically. "I just see things differently." Ashley held her hand up dramatically to her eyes.

"GIVE THAT TO ME!" I shouted. Darlene put her hand on my arm. Cindi and Lauren closed rank behind me.

"Give it back to Jodi," said Darlene. Her voice was low and angry.

Ashley jumped on a bench. Becky and Gloria acted like her bodyguards and wouldn't let me get to her.

Ashley started giggling so hard she could barely speak, as she rifled through my pages.

"That's mine!" I cried, close to tears.

"I know," said Ashley. "But a book is public property."

"IT'S PRIVATE!" I screamed.

"Listen to this," said Ashley, jumping up and down. "I'm like Patrick," she read. "I'm a right-brained, left-handed kid. I'm not stupid."

Ashley collapsed in a heap of giggles. "I'm not stupid!" Ashley started chanting. "I'm not stupid!" Gloria and Becky joined her.

"Cut it out!" shouted Lauren. "You are all such jerks."

"Right-brained? She's pea-brained," said Gloria, reading over Ashley's shoulder. "Look, she even spelled Patrick wrong, 'Patick.'"

"Patick, Patick, Patick!" shrieked Ashley. "Jodi's got a crush on Patick. . . ."

Becky riffed through my pages. She snorted. "Friends," she read. "A friend is like putting ice on a bruise. Ice is cold, but a friend heals. A friend's jokes never wound." Becky tossed the journal back to Ashley.

Ashley swooned back toward the locker. "This is just too, too beautiful for words. A friend is like an ice cube, a melting ice cube. . . ."

"Of course, dum-dum couldn't spell bruise. . . . she spelled it 'bruse' . . . " said Becky.

" 'Bruse' me another ice cube," shouted Ashley.

I pushed Gloria and Becky aside and leaped on Ashley. She tried to put my journal behind her back. I wrestled her for it. I got a few pages, but Ashley wouldn't let go. I pushed her and she fell back against a locker, ripping my notebook. I was ready to punch her.

"Jodi! Be careful!" shouted Darlene. She tried to pull me off Ashley.

"You ripped it!" I yelled. "You — "

"Sorry . . . " said Ashley prissily. She rubbed her arm where I had pushed her. The other girls stood around silently. I think I had scared them with my fury. I know I had scared myself.

Ashley sidled away toward the bathroom. "Boy, she's got some temper," she whispered to Gloria.

I looked down at the ripped notebook in my hand. Only one of the pages was torn. I took the unripped pages and slowly tore them in half. Ashley had been right. I was stupid. I couldn't even spell Patrick right. My words had sounded so stupid read out loud.

"What are you doing?" Lauren screeched.

"It's all trash!" I cried. "I'm stupid, stupid, stupid." Every time I said stupid I ripped out another page.

"Don't!" shouted Cindi.

"Why not?" I ripped out another page. "They're right. I'm dumb."

"You are not!" Lauren grabbed for the journal. I tried to pull it away.

"You can't do this!" yelled Lauren. Lauren's much smaller than me, but somehow she hooked my leg with her foot, and I came crashing down on the carpet, the journal beneath me.

"The Pinecones are fighting! The Pinecones are fighting!" shrieked Ashley. She ran out the door.

Lauren sat on top of me. "You can't rip it all up!" shouted Lauren. "Help!"

Cindi sat on my rear and tried to hold my legs. Darlene tried to reach underneath me to get the journal.

"Let me up!" I grunted. Lauren and Cindi weren't hurting me, but they were heavy.

"No," said Lauren. "Not until you come to your senses."

The door to the locker room swung open. Patrick stuck his head in. "What's going on?" he demanded.

I raised my head. That was all I could lift.

"Nothing," said Lauren sweetly.

"Jodi, are you all right?" asked Patrick.

"We're just practicing a new move," said Darlene. She pushed Patrick out the door. "It's nothing," she said.

Lauren shifted her weight and rolled off me. I sat up. I looked down at the torn pages under my stomach. "Yeah, it's nothing." I mumbled. A whole pile of nothing.

14

You Can't Tell a Book By Its Pages

Lauren started gathering the torn pages. Cindi sat cross-legged at my side.

I closed my eyes for a second.

"Are you okay?" Cindi asked softly.

I leaned back against the locker, trying hard not to cry. I opened my eyes. Lauren was trying to sort out the pages. It looked like she was playing with a jigsaw puzzle of my messy handwriting.

I couldn't trust myself to speak.

Darlene sat down on the bench opposite me. She put her hand on my knee. "I was about to punch Ashley in the nose myself."

"What are you doing, Lauren?" I asked finally.

Lauren looked up from her separate piles. "I'm putting it back together."

"Why? I want it in the garbage."

Lauren didn't answer me. She kept sorting the pages. Cindi got up to help her.

I didn't have the strength to move. "You didn't hurt yourself, did you?" Darlene asked.

"No. Did I hurt Ashley?"

"Unfortunately not very much. That little girl is pond scum in a package," said Darlene.

"Hey," said Lauren, reading one of my torn pages. "You really did describe Becky as a buzzard in a leotard. That's good."

"Give me that," I said, standing up. "I didn't say it was Becky."

"I know," said Lauren. "But it couldn't be anybody else. The way she's always sticking her neck into other people's business."

"The way she loves to hear bad news," added Cindi. "It's a great description. Ms. Assante will love it. She loves . . . what's that word when we use animals to describe people?"

"Anthropomorphic?" asked Lauren. "Or is that the other way around?"

"What do you kids study in that school?" asked Darlene. "I don't know that word."

"Ms. Assante loves *vivid* writing," said Cindi.

She managed to sound just like Ms. Assante. Cindi's a great mimic.

"I can't hand it in," I said. "It's in a million pieces. It's got a zillion spelling mistakes. It's illiterate."

Lauren put down the jagged pieces of paper she was trying to put together.

"So you're just gonna quit on the Pinecones?" she asked.

I blinked. "What does this have to do with the Pinecones? It's just me."

"Oh, yeah?" said Darlene. "You don't think we'd miss you if you didn't come on the trip?"

"It'd be like part of us was gone," said Cindi. "It won't be half as much fun if you're not there."

"And what about Patrick?" asked Lauren. "Are you going to let him down? He *wants* to use you for his demonstration."

I looked at the ripped and torn pages. "Do you really think I can hand this in?" I asked.

"What choice do you have?" asked Lauren. "If you don't, you definitely can't go to Colorado Springs."

"And Ashley gets what she wants. Patrick will use her in the demonstration," said Cindi.

I looked around at Cindi, Darlene, and Lauren. I thought about them. I had been so busy worrying about myself I hadn't realized they would miss me if I didn't go. I was that important to them. I almost started to cry again. "You guys are the best ice cubes a friend ever had," I said.

"Let me at the Scotchtape," said Darlene.

By the time we finished, my journal looked like Frankenstein's first cousin. The pages were all uneven and wrinkled. It was twice as thick from all the tape holding it together. It looked like a book that had been dropped in a bathtub and then put through a shredder.

"Ms. Assante's going to hate this," I said. "She'll never tell Mom that I can go to Colorado Springs."

Lauren handed the book to me. "She always says you can't tell a book by its cover. Just tell her that you can't tell a book by its pages."

"Very funny," I said.

I stuffed the journal back into my knapsack.

Ashley came back into the locker room. She was alone. She looked surprised to see us still there.

Darlene glared at her. Ashley tiptoed over to her locker. "I left something," she said quietly.

I didn't say anything to her. The room was totally silent.

Ashley turned to me. "I'm sorry your notebook got ripped."

"Sorry isn't enough," I said. "It was private, and you knew it."

"Becky told me to read it out loud," whined Ashley. "We knew you kept it in your knapsack."

"If Becky told you to jump off a cliff, would you jump?" Lauren demanded. "You really are a Becky-in-training."

"What does that mean?" Ashley said.

"It means that you'd better not mess with the Pinecones," said Darlene.

We turned our backs on her and left the locker room together. Sorry wasn't enough, and I wouldn't have changed places with Ashley for all her talent.

I had something better than talent. I had friends who wouldn't let me quit on myself. That was worth all the ice cubes in Alaska.

15

I'm Not Doing This for My Health

Lauren and Cindi had to practically push me toward the front of the class after school. "Give it to her now," hissed Lauren.

"Get it over with," whispered Cindi.

Ms. Assante was grading papers. If she heard us whispering in the aisle she pretended not to.

Cindi gave me a final push and they left the room. Ms. Assante looked up. "Jodi," she said. "Do you have your journal for me?"

I dug into my knapsack and brought out my journal. It looked even worse than I remembered.

Ms. Assante turned it over in her hands. She frowned. "I thought this was going to be something you cared about," she said.

"I *did*."

Ms. Assante scowled. "Did. Past tense?"

"Very past tense," I repeated. I fled the room, leaving my fate on her desk, a ripped up, fouled up, misshapen, misspelled disaster.

Cindi and Lauren were waiting for me outside the door. "She thinks it's disgusting," I snapped. "Don't ask me about it."

Cindi and Lauren knew enough to be quiet. I stared out the window on the bus to Patrick's.

As soon as I walked into the gym, Darlene knew something was wrong. "Did you hand in your journal?" she asked.

"I handed it in, and she thought it was a mess."

"That was just the outside," argued Lauren. "She hasn't even read it yet."

"Lauren, if you tell me one more time to look on the bright side, I'll clobber you," I said.

Lauren buttoned her lip.

We went out to the gym. Patrick was working with Becky on the beam.

It was very weird. He kept repeating her name in a loud voice. I watched her as we warmed up. She did a beautiful back walkover. Her hips were perfectly square to the beam, and she didn't wobble once. Patrick's hands were ready to guide her, but he didn't even touch her.

"Becky! Becky!" he almost shouted. I couldn't tell if he was mad at her or what.

She took a deep breath and did a front aerial on the beam. A no-hands cartwheel. In order to do that on the beam, you absolutely have to be rock-solid.

"Stupendous," said Patrick, his voice pitched low. He gave her a thumbs-up sign.

Becky did a back somersault dismount. Patrick only had to lightly tap her on the back to help her get around.

"Superb," he said. I couldn't believe that she could do a front aerial on the beam.

"She is something else," said Darlene, joining us for our warm-ups.

"You can say that again," muttered Cindi. "She's so good, she's like from another planet."

My hamstrings hurt as I was doing my warm-up. Sometimes you can tell right from the warm-up that it's going to be a lousy day.

Patrick gathered us around. "I want to work on your attention span," he said. "I've been reading a book by Coach Joseph Massimo. I want to try a technique I found in his book. You're going to face lots of distractions at the mini-camp. I want each of you to run through your beam routine, but at random moments, I'm going to call out your name. Don't stop when you hear your name. Try to concentrate and keep going."

Beam is my least favorite event, anyhow. Even on the best of days, I am not known for my control.

"This is going to be easy for me," Cindi said. "My brothers are always shouting my name."

She did a handstand mount. Then just as she was about to do her leap, Patrick called out "Cindi!"

She wobbled, but she stayed on the beam. She completed the entire exercise without falling off once.

"Excellent," said Patrick.

Lauren had a harder time. She fell off the first time that Patrick called her name, but then after she remounted, she did fine.

"All right, Jodi, your turn," said Patrick.

My mount was a "tuck" in which I jump from the vaulting board in a tuck position onto the beam.

I wobbled and had to use my hands to steady myself, but I didn't fall off.

I did a body wave. Patrick called out "Jodi!" The sound of my own name made me fall off. I jumped to the side of the beam.

"Sorry," I said.

"It's okay," said Patrick. "The point of the exercise is to make you concentrate."

I mounted again. I was doing the simplest move when Patrick yelled my name again. I couldn't help myself. I fell off again. And again. All in all, I fell off six times.

"Jodi, you aren't concentrating at all," said Patrick. "Use your brain."

"It's stuck on the right side," I said, trying to make a joke.

"I'm not doing this for my health," said Patrick, something that all adults say when they're annoyed. Why do they believe we think they're doing it for their health? It's such a stupid complaint.

"I know," I mumbled. "You're doing it for my own good. I'm sick and tired of everybody doing things for my own good."

Patrick looked angry. "Jodi, don't talk back to me. Go do fifteen laps around the gym until you calm down."

"Yes, sir," I said.

I did my laps, but I didn't have to like them. I saw Patrick start to work with Ashley. Little Miss Perfect. They would make a perfect team at the demonstration. They didn't need me, anyhow. It was a good thing. Because I knew my luck. I had seen the way that Ms. Assante had been shocked at the condition of my journal. She thought it was just another example of my disrespect. No way was she going to tell my mother that I had fulfilled our contract.

I didn't care anyway. Did I?

16

So Do I,
So Do I

The next day after school, Mom met me outside of Ms. Assante's room. She put her arm around me. "You nervous?" she asked.

"It's worse than a meet," I admitted. I hadn't told Mom what had happened to my journal. That seemed like tattling.

Ms. Assante called us into her room. She held my journal in her hand. "Ms. Sutton," she said. "This is Jodi's journal." She handed it to Mom.

Mom turned my journal over. "It looks like it's been through the wars," said Mom. "Jodi, how could you hand in something like this. It's so disrespectful."

"No . . . no," said Ms. Assante, "that's not what

I mean." She leaned across her desk and took back my journal. "I mean look at how many pages Jodi wrote. Some days she wrote as many as five pages."

"Once I got started sometimes I just couldn't stop . . . " I admitted.

"And the writing's so colorful," said Ms. Assante. "I knew, Jodi, you had a vivid imagination . . . but a buzzard in a leotard. . . ."

I coughed. "Can we skip that part?" I asked.

"I will," said Ms. Assante. "But may I read the part you wrote about, what do you call it? 'spilling'?"

"Spotting," I said. "Yeah, I guess you can read that part." It was something I had written the last day.

"Listen to this, Ms. Sutton," said Ms. Assante. "Jodi wrote, 'People think that I will try anything. But I get scared. Yet Patrick's hand on my back makes me want to go for it. Turning in the air, I see his feet, and I know I'll land. Turning in space with a helping hand.' "

"Dumb, huh?" I said.

"No, no," said Ms. Assante. "It's so vivid. The way you talk about your coach made me think about myself as a teacher. I loved that passage."

"Patrick finds Jodi a delight to coach," said my mother. "With his help, she's blossoming as a gymnast in ways she never did back in St. Louis."

"She's blossoming as a student even more," said Ms. Assante. "May I read just a little more," she asked, "about Patrick?"

I nodded. I could feel myself blushing. "I don't even spell his name right," I said.

"You have a million different ways of spelling gymnastics," said Ms. Assante. "That's not the point. Let me read your mother another excerpt."

" 'I watch someone like Ashley and I want to hate her, but every day Ashley tests herself to be the best she can be. I don't. If I keep making jokes I think nobody will know that I want to be good.' "

Ms. Assante closed my notebook. "I learned more about you from this journal, more to admire and respect, than I have in six months of working with you in the classroom."

I chewed my fingernail. I really couldn't believe what I was hearing. She liked it. Did that mean I was going to get to go to Colorado Springs? I thought about Ashley and how I had almost thrown the whole thing into the garbage. I would have if it hadn't been for the other Pinecones.

"I envy Patrick," said Ms. Assante. "He sounds like a wonderful teacher."

"The way I acted yesterday," I said, "he probably wants to use Ashley in the demonstration." I hated the thought of Ashley getting to show off in front of my sister.

Mom coughed. "Ms. Assante, I guess you're telling me you think that Jodi lived up to her end of the bargain," she said.

"Definitely," said Ms. Assante.

Mom took a piece of paper out of her purse. "I think I'd like to sign this in front of you and Jodi."

"What's that?" I asked.

"It's your permission slip to go to the mini-camp."

I breathed a deep sigh. "You mean it?" I asked.

Mom nodded. "Haven't you heard Ms. Assante? She's proud of you," she said. "So am I."

I picked up my ripped-and-scotchtaped-together journal. "You don't know how close this came to ending up in the garbage pail," I muttered.

Ms. Asssante stared at me. "What do you mean?" she asked.

"Nothing," I said. "Some things are private." I picked up the journal and stuffed it in my knapsack.

"You have to keep writing in your journal, just

like the other students," said Ms. Assante.

"I know," I said.

"Besides," said Ms. Assante. "I want to find out how things go in Colorado Springs."

"So do I," I said. "So do I."

17

Air Force Blue
Is Tacky

"NINETY-NINE BOTTLES OF BEER ON THE WALL," sang out Cindi.

"I don't think that's a good song to sing," said Lauren. We were just a few minutes outside Colorado Springs. It was a beautiful sunny day, and we had been singing all the way down.

That is, most of us had been singing. Lauren had been up front, sitting next to Patrick so she wouldn't get carsick.

We turned into the Olympic Center. I had expected something a lot fancier. There were flags out front, but it was in a residential area with little wooden houses all around it.

The Evergreen team stayed in one dormitory

room but we four Pinecones got beds next to each other. We made sure we were on the opposite side of the room from Becky, Ashley, and their gang.

Patrick told us to store our duffel bags and meet him in the gymnasium.

The gymnasium made you realize that all the money had been spent on the inside. It had every piece of equipment you could imagine. The gymnasium was decorated with flags representing different countries. It had a special floor that gave extra bounce to our tumbling runs.

In one room an entire set of men's and women's apparatuses was placed in the middle of a huge pit with small blue and white squares of soft foam, so that we could try things we couldn't try at home without hurting ourselves.

The girls working out on the apparatus were amazing. Some of them made our archrivals the Atomic Amazons look like beginners.

As we started working out in the area assigned to us, we realized that at least some of the others were intermediates and even beginners like us.

I worked out with the other Pinecones. I loved the pit. Falling into it was really like flying. With the pit I could try a back somersault dismount from the beam.

"Hey," said Darlene. "Someone's waving at you."

I looked up in the stands and saw my sister sitting with a group of her friends.

I ran over to her. She put her arm around me. She looked terrific in her powder-blue uniform.

I introduced her to the other Pinecones.

Patrick came over to us. "Hi," said Jennifer, sticking out her hand and shaking hands with Patrick as if they were equals. "I'm glad to meet you."

"I've heard some terrific things about you from your mother," said Patrick. "I'd love to see you work out."

"I'm here to watch Jodi," said Jennifer.

"You're going to be an astronaut!" said Cindi. "That's so cool. My dad's a pilot. I'd love to be an astronaut someday, too."

"Hold on," said Jennifer. "I'm a long way from being an astronaut yet."

"But you've studied weightlessness, haven't you?" asked Darlene. "I'd like to have no weight."

"It's different, all right," said Jennifer.

"How do you get into the Air Force Academy?" asked Ashley.

"You've got to have incredible grades," said Lauren. "And then you have to be nominated by your congressman. It's a great honor."

I moved aside so my friends could get closer to Jennifer. Everybody always has wanted to be close to Jennifer. I bit my nail.

Darlene stepped close to me. "Your sister's great," she said. "She is prettier in real life than in her picture."

"I know," I admitted.

"You know, it's hard for me sometimes, too," Darlene said.

"What?" I asked.

"Everyone always makes a fuss about my dad," she said. "It's like a sixth sense with me. I know when someone else feels like I do."

"My sister is worse than Ashley," I said.

Darlene stared at me. I tried to explain. "Jennifer was as good as Ashley when she was nine years old, but she's also always been nice."

"She's not perfect," said Darlene.

I looked at her. "She's not?" I asked. From where I stood, Jennifer seemed pretty perfect to me. She was smart, she was a great gymnast, and all my friends couldn't wait to get closer to her.

Darlene shook her head. "She doesn't look good in powder-blue," Darlene said. "That uniform looks tacky on her."

I giggled. Trust Darlene to think that the Air

Force uniforms were tacky. But Darlene had made me feel better.

"Come on," I said. "I want you to meet her, but don't tell her she doesn't look good in Air Force blue."

18

There's More to Life Than Being Perfect

"Are you ready?" Patrick whispered to me. I looked up at the stands. I had to show my sister what I could do. The stands were full of other coaches and gymnasts. Patrick and I stood alone on the floor. Just the two of us.

The announcer spoke on the loudspeaker. "Now we have Patrick Harmon from the Evergreen Gymnastics Academy. Patrick is one of our younger coaches. Lots of you may remember him from his days of competing with the University of Denver.

"He is going to show us some of his spotting techniques with a young gymnast from an illustrious gymnastics background, Jodi Sutton. Her mother was on our World Cup team and is now a coach at Patrick's Evergreen Academy. Her sister is well known here in Colorado Springs where she attends the United States Air Force Academy."

I ducked my head and stared at the tumbling mat. Why did they have to do that? I wondered. Today was my day to shine. Why did they have to mention Jennifer?

"Would Jennifer Sutton take a bow," said the announcer.

Jennifer stood up and waved to the crowd. I could see her smiling at me. She gave me a special wave. I waved back. I'd have to do my best. It would be dumb not to.

"Sorry about that," Patrick whispered to me. "They asked me for your family background."

Patrick took the microphone. "Jodi is one of my more enthusiastic gymnasts," he said. "I can always count on her to be willing to try anything. She picks up things very quickly, and we have been working on the difference between a back handspring and a back somersault." He coughed. His voice was higher than usual. He really was nervous. "We will try to demonstrate the different spotting needed for a handspring, and then a back somie."

I went to the edge of the mat. I did a warm-up

of a few cartwheels. The crowd applauded just for them.

Then Patrick stood in the middle of the mat, and I began my tumbling run. I felt confident because I knew Patrick was strong enough to catch me in the air.

"Think height," I told myself. I pictured the run in my head, then I took off.

I ran six short steps as quickly as I could, then I threw myself into the roundoff, and as soon as I punched up, I leaned backwards, slinking into my handsprings. Patrick spotted me through my handsprings.

Then it was time for my next pass. "Up!" Patrick whispered. I came out of my last handspring and leaned forward, trying to "block" all the backward momentum and use it. I used all my energy to reach for the ceiling. I felt Patrick's hand underneath me. Then I grabbed my knees, and I seemed to float around. Patrick's hand on my back made me feel weightless. As I spun around, I could see the tips of his toes. I straightened out and he helped lower me to the ground. My hands were high in a victory salute.

The crowd applauded. For me! Patrick and I moved to the side while the next coach and gymnast got ready for their demonstration. It had all happened so quickly. I wanted to go out there and shine again.

"Jodi, you were terrific," said Patrick.

I grinned.

"It felt easy," I said.

"Well, I was sweating," said Patrick. "I was so nervous."

I didn't let Patrick know that I could tell. "I didn't want to foul up in front of my peers," said Patrick. "You made me look good." He put my warm-up jacket around my shoulders. "Come on," he said. "Let's go watch the other demonstrations."

We made our way up to our seats. Lauren, Cindi, and Darlene were still standing and clapping. So was my sister.

I gave them all a high five.

"You were really good," said Lauren. "I would have been scared to death in front of all those people."

"I knew Patrick would catch me if I fell," I said.

Then I asked Jennifer for my knapsack. She handed it to me.

I took out my new journal. While the feeling was fresh I wanted to write down what Patrick had said to me. "You made me look good," I wrote. "Even a coach or a teacher gets nervous."

"What are you doing?" asked Jennifer.

"Writing in my journal," I said.

"Is this something new?" Jennifer asked.

I nodded. "I learn a lot when I write," I said.

"That's terrific," said Jennifer. "I never was very good at writing. I was much better at math."

"You've got to keep at it," I said. I grinned at her. Then I picked up my pen. "Even Jennifer isn't perfect," I wrote. "But I'm the kind of girl who can learn. I'd rather be a learner than perfect. There's more to life than being perfect."

I glanced over at Ashley. "Little Miss Perfect. I wouldn't be her for anything," I wrote in my journal.

Then I put it away. "What did you write?" Darlene asked me.

"There's more to life than being perfect," I said.

"You can say that again," said Darlene.

"What's that?" asked Lauren.

I repeated my line. Lauren grinned and whispered it to Cindi.

"What are you all whispering about?" asked Ashley. She really sounded like a little kid.

"Nothing," I said. "You'd have to be a Pinecone to understand."

"Pinecones aren't perfect," whined Ashley.

The four of us cracked up. We almost fell off the bench we were laughing so hard. Believe me, there's a lot more to life than being perfect.

There's being a Pinecone.

WIN A BRAND NEW GYMNASTICS WARDROBE

Announcing...

THE GYMNASTS CONTEST!

Flip for gymnastics! You're invited to enter The Gymnasts Contest—YOU can win a fantastic gymnastics wardrobe, including a duffel bag, valued at $100.00! It's easy! Just complete the coupon below and return by December 31, 1988.

Watch for *The Winner* #4
coming in January wherever you buy books!